# Journey to Antarctica

By Julie Haydon

**PM Nonfiction**
part of the Rigby PM Collection

U.S. edition © 2001 Rigby
a division of Reed Elsevier Inc.
1000 Hart Road
Barrington, IL 60010–2627
www.rigby.com

Text © Julie Haydon 2001
Illustrations © Nelson Thomson Learning 2001
Originally published in Australia by Nelson Thomson Learning

06 05 04 03 02 01
10 9 8 7 6 5 4 3 2 1

Journey to Antarctica
ISBN  0 7578 1169 8

Designed by Karen Mayo
Illustrations by Alan Laver
Photographs: ANT Photo Library, pp. 13, 14-15 (background), 15 (inset), 19 (sea ice), / © Dave
Watts, p. 21 (top); Australian Picture Library/ Corbis/ © Ann Hawthorne, p. 31, / © Hulton-Deutsch
Collection, p. 30 (Fuchs & Hillary), / © Peter Johnson, p. 4, 19 (floes), 26 (crabeater), 27 (weddell &
leopard), 28 (adelie), / © Wolfgang Kaehler, pp. 2-3, 32-3, 19 (pack ice), 28 (chinstrap & emperor), /
© Rick Price, pp. 9, 22, / © Chris Ranier, p. 19 (top), / © Galen Rowell, pp. 5, 11, 18 (top), 20 (right), /
© Kevin Schafer, p. 18 (bottom), / © Randy Wells, p. 28 (gentoo); Ken Green/ Hedgehog House
New Zealand, p. 27 (ross); Tim Higham/ Antarctica N.Z./ Hedgehog House New Zealand, p. 17
(top); Hulton-Getty, p. 30 (Shackleton & Wilson, Byrd); Colin Monteath/ Hedgehog House New
Zealand, pp. 12-13, 19 (pancake ice); By permission of the National Library of Australia, p. 30 (top);
Nathaniel B. Palmer/ Hedgehog House New Zealand, p. 29; Photolibrary.com, cover; Galen Rowell/
Hedgehog House New Zealand, p. 25; Chris Rudge/ Hedgehog House New Zealand, p. 21
(bottom); United States National Science Foundation, pp. 13, 17 (bottom),
20 (left), 23.
Printed in China through Midas Printing (Asia) Ltd

# Contents

# CHAPTER 1

# Off to Antarctica!

| Subject: | I'm off to Antarctica! | |
|---|---|---|
| Date: | October 2 10:25 | Send |

Dear Luke,

I am so excited I can barely type. Your big sister is going to Antarctica! It's the coldest, windiest, highest *continent* on earth. It's also the driest. In fact, as so little rain and snow falls in Antarctica, it's officially a desert!

I'm going to be living on a research station during the Antarctic summer and working as a botanist on this barren continent.

And barren is definitely the word! This ice-covered landmass may be the fifth largest continent on earth, but it has no trees or *arable* land, no land mammals, no reptiles, no amphibians, and no permanent human population.

Despite Antarctica being the most inhospitable place on earth, scientists from all over the world go there to work — and best of all, they share their knowledge with each other.

I leave in two months!

Love, Bridget

**Although penguins are the most well known of the Antarctic birds, other bird species, like this giant petrel, make the ice-covered continent and its waters home.**

Dear Luke,

Thanks for the bon voyage e-card! I leave in four days, so I've been incredibly busy preparing for the trip. Here are some of the things I've had to do:

1) Learn basic survival skills and how to operate special tools, equipment, and vehicles. (The training will continue in Antarctica.)

2) Have a medical examination. (If I was a doctor going to Antarctica, I'd have to have my appendix removed — can you guess why?)

3) Study the land and history of Antarctica.

4) Plan the work I will be doing in Antarctica.

5) Get fit for special polar clothing that will keep me warm and dry.

Love, Bridget

**Typical expeditioner clothing includes thermal underwear, woolen shirts, windproof overalls and parkas, caps, boots, gloves, and goggles. Layers of clothing _insulate_ the body by keeping body heat in.**

P.S. Did you figure it out?

If I was a doctor going to Antarctica, I'd have to have my appendix removed beforehand because I couldn't operate on myself if my appendix ruptured — and there is only one doctor on the station!

# CHAPTER 2

# Geography and Natural History

| Subject: | Map of Antarctica |
|---|---|
| Date: | November 30 15:14 |

**Send**

Dear Luke,

Here is the map of Antarctica you asked for.

Love, Bridget

WEDDELL SEA

Ronne
Ice Shelf

Rothera
(U.K.)

WEST
ANTARCTICA

SOUTHERN OCEAN

## How Big Is Antarctica?

The continent of Antarctica covers an area of more than 5.5 million square miles. Imagine a continent nearly twice the size of Australia, or one-and-a-half times the size of the United States. In winter, Antarctica's ice spreads northward over the Southern Ocean, covering an additional 8 million square miles.

## The Southern Ocean

The southern parts of the Atlantic, Indian, and Pacific Oceans form the Southern Ocean, which surrounds Antarctica. It is the world's wildest and most dangerous ocean to cross. In summer, when the sea ice melts, the Southern Ocean is a rich source of food for Antarctica's wildlife.

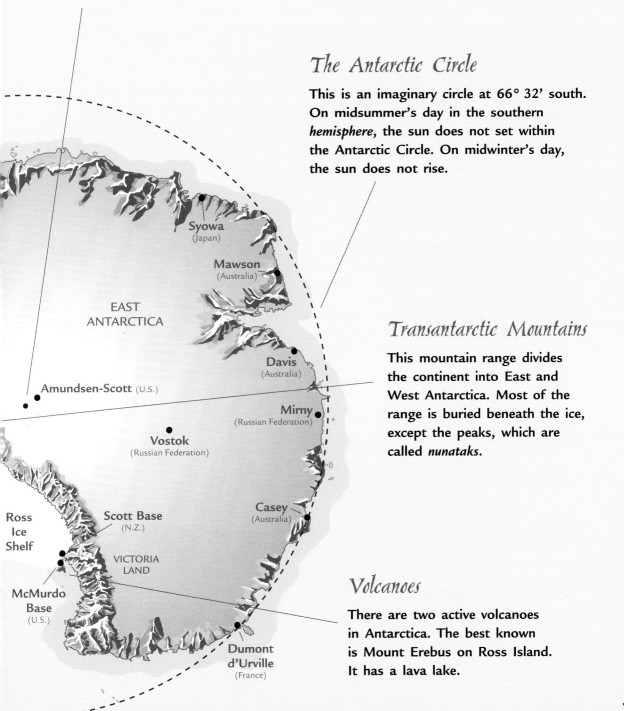

## The Geographic South Pole

The geographic South Pole marks the earth's southernmost point. It is an imaginary point situated at 90° south.

## The Antarctic Circle

This is an imaginary circle at 66° 32' south. On midsummer's day in the southern *hemisphere*, the sun does not set within the Antarctic Circle. On midwinter's day, the sun does not rise.

## Transantarctic Mountains

This mountain range divides the continent into East and West Antarctica. Most of the range is buried beneath the ice, except the peaks, which are called *nunataks*.

## Volcanoes

There are two active volcanoes in Antarctica. The best known is Mount Erebus on Ross Island. It has a lava lake.

Syowa
(Japan)

Mawson
(Australia)

EAST
ANTARCTICA

Davis
(Australia)

Amundsen-Scott (U.S.)

Mirny
(Russian Federation)

Vostok
(Russian Federation)

Ross
Ice
Shelf

Scott Base
(N.Z.)

Casey
(Australia)

VICTORIA
LAND

McMurdo
Base
(U.S.)

Dumont
d'Urville
(France)

Dear Luke,

Thanks for your questions. I've got a few minutes, so I thought I'd try and answer them. We're off tomorrow!

## How Did Antarctica Form?

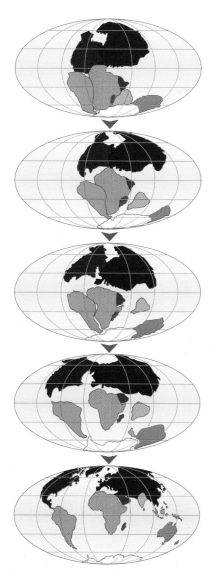

Antarctica was once part of a huge landmass known as Gondwana. Plants and animals thrived in its mild climate.

About 60 million years ago, Gondwana broke up and Australia, India, New Zealand, Africa, South America, and Antarctica drifted toward their present positions.

Several million years ago, the earth began to cool. Antarctica was now a cold and isolated continent. Strong winds blowing over the Southern Ocean brought moisture, which fell as snow over Antarctica. Unable to melt, the snow stayed frozen and Antarctica's icecap formed.

The ancient Greeks believed in the existence of an unknown southern land, or Terra Australis Incognita, as it later became known in Latin, but Antarctica was not discovered until the nineteenth century.

# Why Is Antarctica So Cold?

The effect of the sun's rays is weakest at the North and South Poles. From March to September, when the South Pole is turned away from the sun, it receives no direct sunlight. From September to March, when the South Pole faces the sun, it has continuous daylight. Even then, the ice covering Antarctica's landmass does not melt. This is because cloudy skies prevent much of the sunlight from reaching Antarctica's surface. The light and heat that do reach the surface are reflected off the bright white ice. Antarctica is a high continent, with an average elevation of 7,500 feet above sea level, and this also keeps temperatures low.

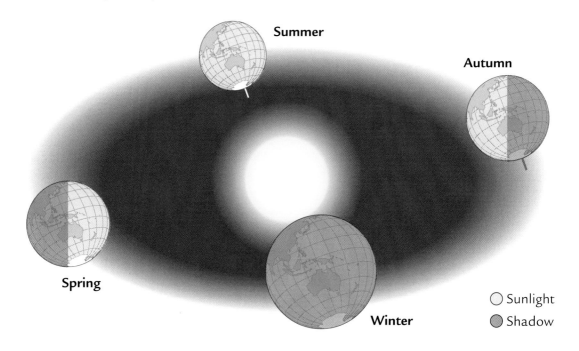

# Some Facts About Antarctic Temperatures

- **The lowest temperature ever recorded was -130°F.**
- **The winter temperature inland is often below -58°F.**
- **The summer temperature inland is often below -22°F.**
- **The coastal temperatures can be up to 86°F warmer than inland temperatures.**

## Does the Sun Set at the South Pole?

During a year at the South Pole, there is only one sunrise and one sunset. The sun rises in September and stays above the horizon for six months until it sets in March. It remains below the horizon for the next six months. The reverse occurs at the North Pole.

Luke, remember I am writing just about the South Pole, not the entire continent of Antarctica. As you move northward from the South Pole toward the Antarctic Circle, you experience fewer days of continuous summer daylight and winter darkness.

Love, Bridget

# CHAPTER 3

# The Journey

| Subject: | The journey has begun |
|----------|-----------------------|
| Date: | December 7 09:37 |

Dear Luke,

It's my fifth day aboard an *icebreaker*. We are crossing the partially frozen Southern Ocean on our way to Antarctica.

The icebreaker is almost 312 feet long and is packed with expeditioners, crew, and cargo. It has six decks, with a gymnasium, a bar, and even a helicopter deck. The ship also functions as a marine research vessel, so there are laboratories, underwater equipment, special computers, a fish freezer, and a darkroom on board.

**An icebreaker has a strengthened hull and is specially designed to travel through ice-choked waters.**

It is very cold and windy, and the temperature is falling. The world around me is the blue and white of sky, clouds, sea, and ice. There are albatrosses, petrels, and other birds flying behind the ship. This morning, we sailed through an enormous patch of the tiny pink *crustaceans* called "krill."

Krill are shrimp-like crustaceans, which form the basic diet of many Antarctic creatures, such as whales, seals, penguins, and other seabirds. It is estimated that 600 million million krill live in the Southern Ocean.

But it's the icebergs that dazzle me. One was a brilliant blue! They are becoming larger and more common the closer we get to Antarctica. They appear as yellow dots on the ship's radar screen.

Yesterday we began moving through sea ice. The sound of it breaking under the weight of the ship is amazing! Did you know that if all of Antarctica's ice was to melt, the world's oceans would rise by over 200 feet, flooding our coastal cities?

Love, Bridget

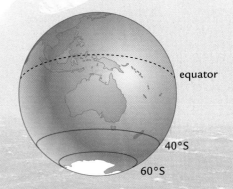

The areas of ocean between the latitudes of 40° and 60° south are known as the "roaring forties," "furious fifties," and "screaming sixties" because of the strong winds that blow there.

P.S. Two helicopters have just taken off from the helicopter deck. The icebreaker is surrounded by thick pack ice and is having difficulty getting through. The pilots are going to search for open water. The helicopters always fly in pairs, so if one gets into trouble and is forced to land, the other can perform a rescue.

# CHAPTER 4

# *Arrival*

| Subject: | Arrival | |
|----------|---------|---|
| Date: | December 11 10:21 | **Send** |

Dear Luke,

I have arrived in Antarctica! After so many days of seeing ocean and ice, it was strange to look out the porthole and see people and vehicles again. They came from the research station to welcome us and unload the ship's cargo. Everything humans need to survive in Antarctica must be brought in — food, medicine, fuel, tools, clothing, mail, building materials, even vehicles.

**During winter, only a small number of expeditioners stay in Antarctica. In summer, when opportunities for research are greater, expeditioner numbers increase.**

It can take several days to unload and reload an icebreaker. Bad weather can disrupt or stop the operation entirely.

The cargo is being unloaded with the help of the ship's crane and placed onto barges. Once on land, it is transported to the research station by truck. Later, the ship will be loaded with anything that needs to be taken out of Antarctica, and the expeditioners who are going home will board it.

It is bitterly cold, -20°F, and the wind has an edge like a knife — in summer! Even so, I decided to walk to the research station where I will be living for the next three months, rather than take a ride in a truck.

My new life on this icy continent has begun.

Love, Bridget

# CHAPTER 5
# The Research Station

Dear Luke,

It was great speaking to you and Mom and Dad on the phone yesterday.

I am typing this on the computer in my room at the research station. The station is modern, comfortable, and warm. Its steel frame is built on a concrete foundation and it has metal-covered insulated wall panels and *triple-glazed* windows. A blizzard is blowing outside, yet I am sitting here in jeans and a shirt.

There are 40 permanent bases in Antarctica run by various nations. The longest continuously operating station within the Antarctic Circle is Australia's Mawson, which was opened in 1954.

Guess˙ what is one of Antarctica's most precious resources? Water. Antarctica might hold 90% of the world's ice and 60-70% of the world's fresh water, but it takes valuable fuel to melt the ice and heat the water for human use.

Despite the station's comforts, Antarctica can be a strange and hostile place. The research station has a boundary and I must get permission to journey beyond it.

Love, Bridget

P.S. At the stations, the risk of fire is very high, due to the dry, windy conditions. If a fire does occur, there are no stores where replacement items can be bought or hotels for people to stay in. So every station has a separate store of food, in case of emergencies.

Norwegian explorer Carsten Borchgrevink and his party of nine men and 75 dogs were the first to spend a winter in Antarctica in 1899. They brought wooden huts with them on their ship, but almost lost the huts to fire (started by a candle) and ferocious winds. Dogs are no longer permitted in Antarctica.

P.P.S. In my spare time at the research station, I can:

- Read (there's a library)
- Watch videos or go to the movies
- Play billiards, table tennis, or darts in the recreation room
- Listen to music or learn an instrument
- Meet friends at the station's restaurant
- Go cross-country skiing
- Take photographs
- Go on field trips

*This is my room!*

And, best of all, these activities are free.
I don't need any money while I'm in Antarctica!

# CHAPTER 6

# Ice, Ice, and More Ice

**Subject:** Ice everywhere!

**Date:** December 29 21:54

Send

Dear Luke,

There is so much ice here in Antarctica! I thought I'd write about the different forms it can take.

Happy New Year to the whole family.

Love, Bridget

## Ice Sheet *(left)*

Antarctica is covered by a dome-like ice sheet made of compacted snow and ice. The ice sheet is more than 13,000 feet thick in places and literally weighs Antarctica down. Scientists have estimated that if the ice sheet was to melt, the rock beneath would rise by over 2,200 feet. Only about 2% of Antarctica's land is free of ice.

## Glaciers *(right)*

Slow-moving rivers of ice called glaciers flow off the ice sheet. The world's largest glacier, Lambert Glacier, is in Antarctica. It is 25 miles wide and 248 miles long.

## Ice Shelves *(above)*

Floating ice sheets attached to land are called ice shelves. The two largest ice shelves in Antarctica are the Ross Ice Shelf in the Ross Sea, and the Ronne Ice Shelf in the Weddell Sea. Their cliffs of ice, which are known as fronts, rear up over 164 feet above the sea.

## Icebergs

When the glaciers and ice shelves reach the sea, chunks of ice break off, becoming icebergs. Usually only one-ninth of an iceberg is visible above the water.

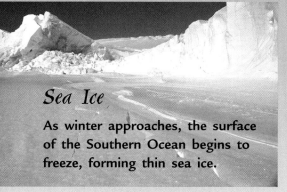

## Sea Ice

As winter approaches, the surface of the Southern Ocean begins to freeze, forming thin sea ice.

## Pancake Ice

The sea water buffets the ice. The ice breaks into pieces shaped like plates, or pancakes.

## Pack Ice *(below)*

As the temperature continues to drop, the whole surface of the ocean freezes. This pack ice can be several yards thick. Most of it will melt in summer.

## Floes

The pack ice breaks into large pieces of ice called floes.

19

# CHAPTER 7

# Living in Antarctica

| Subject: | Everyday life |
| --- | --- |
| Date: | January 10 16:22 |

**Send**

Dear Luke,

## Friends

I have been living at the station for a month now and I have made many new friends. Because expeditioners live so closely together, away from our families and homes, it is important that we are tolerant and respect each other's privacy. Not all the people here are scientists. For the station to function, it needs engineers, carpenters, plumbers, mechanics, technicians, electricians, a doctor, a chef, and a station leader.

**Despite the cold, people in Antarctica must protect their eyes and faces from the sunlight reflecting off the ice and snow.**

This scientist is using a special balloon to help gather information on the Antarctic climate.

## Energy

Electricity for the station is generated by diesel engines. Hundreds of thousands of gallons of fuel for the engines are brought in on icebreakers. Without the fuel, there would be no light, heat, or power at the station.

## Vehicles

The most popular vehicle is the quad. It is a four-wheel bike. There are also motorized toboggans, large all-terrain vehicles, and numerous bulldozers, tractors, and trucks for use around the station.

I have to go. Tonight I am on "slushy" duty, which means I have to set the tables in the dining room and help the cook prepare the meals. Everyone takes a turn doing other chores, including cleaning and taking out the garbage.

Love, Bridget

# CHAPTER 8
## Science and Antarctica

Dear Luke,

I thought you might like to know about the scientists who come to Antarctica to conduct research.

- **Botanists** (like me!) study Antarctica's plants. I've been away for the last few days on a field trip, measuring samples of lichen and moss.

- **Glaciologists** study Antarctica's ice.

- **Biologists** study Antarctica's marine, land, and lake creatures.

Few plants can grow in Antarctica's harsh climate. Botanists study how Antarctic plants, such as this moss, adapt to their environment.

- **Meteorologists** study the atmosphere and weather, including the effects of global pollution on the *ozone layer*.

- **Geologists** study the earth's crust on Antarctica's landmass and beneath the Southern Ocean.

- **Oceanographers** study the Southern Ocean.

- **Medical researchers** study the effects of living in Antarctica on the human body.

Love, Bridget

**Glaciologists take a sample of ice from Antarctica's ice sheet. The ice sheet has formed over hundreds of thousands of years and contains trapped chemicals, dust, and gas. By studying the ice, scientists can learn about the earth's climatic changes and the world-wide spread of industrial pollution.**

Send

Hello Sixth Grade students,

Thank you all for your lovely e-mails. (A special hello to my brother, Luke.) It's wonderful that you're studying Antarctica at school, and yes, I'd love to come and speak to you all when I return.

You asked about the Antarctic *Treaty* — here's what I can tell you about it:

## The Antarctic Treaty:

- was signed by twelve nations in 1959 and came into effect in 1961. The original signatory nations were Argentina, Australia, Belgium, Chile, France, Japan, New Zealand, Norway, South Africa, the United Kingdom, the United States and the Soviet Union (now the Russian Federation)

- states that Antarctica should be used only for peaceful purposes

- guarantees freedom and exchange of scientific research and personnel

- bans nuclear explosions, military activity, and the disposal of radioactive waste

- allows for inspections of any nation's stations/equipment and supply ships/aircraft

- ensures freedom of access to all areas of Antarctica

- had 44 nation members in 2001

Before the signing of the Antarctic Treaty, seven nations had laid claim to parts of Antarctica. The intent of the Treaty was to freeze all territorial claims, to promote international scientific cooperation, and to protect the Antarctic environment.

The Treaty has brought about a 50-year ban on commercial mining in Antarctica and numerous conservation agreements to protect the continent's flora and fauna.

From, Bridget Allan

**In 1991, the members of the Antarctic Treaty signed an agreement known as the Madrid Protocol. It names Antarctica as a natural reserve, devoted to peace and science, and sets strict rules for waste storage, disposal, and removal. Most waste is collected and removed via ship (kitchen waste is incinerated first). The waste in this photograph has been compacted, and is ready for removal.**

# CHAPTER 9
## Seals and Penguins

| | |
|---|---|
| Subject: | Seals and penguins |
| Date: | February 25 07:07 |

Send

Dear Luke,

Here are photos of some of Antarctica's seals and penguins.

Seals are marine mammals, and during Antarctica's winter, they escape the cold by taking to the sea. Some stay under the ice, and others head north to return in the spring.

Penguins are birds that can swim but cannot fly. Their bodies are well-adapted to the cold.

Love, Bridget

Crabeater seals (left) spend their time in the sea or on ice floes. They eat krill, not crabs, and are the most numerous large mammal in the world after humans.

Leopard seals (below) are fast and strong. They have a varied diet, ranging from krill to penguins and young crabeater seals.

Weddell seals (above) are skilful divers. They eat deep-water fish, krill, and squid. During winter, which they spend in the water, they keep breathing holes open in the thick ice by gnawing at the holes' edges with their large teeth.

Ross seals were only discovered in 1840 and are rarely seen. They live on and beneath the pack ice and eat squid and fish.

Adélie penguins (above) breed in the far south and often have to walk long distances over sea ice to reach their nesting sites. They lay two eggs in nests made of pebbles. The eggs hatch at the start of summer.

Emperor penguins (above) are the largest penguins and the only native warm-blooded creatures to spend winter in Antarctica. In late autumn, a female lays a single egg which the male places on top of its feet and covers with a flap of skin. The male protects the egg for the entire winter. When the chick hatches in spring, the female returns and the male leaves to feed.

Chinstrap penguins (above) have a distinctive black line of feathers under their chins. They can be aggressive toward each other and build their nests out of pecking range. Chinstraps and Adélies feed mainly on krill.

Gentoo penguins (left) have a white patch above each eye. They feed on krill and fish.

# CHAPTER 10

# Homeward Bound

| Subject: | The end of an adventure |
|---|---|
| Date: | March 6 22:43 |

Send

Dear Luke,

Tomorrow I board a ship for home. Autumn has begun here and my time in Antarctica is over. I will be happy to see you, the rest of the family, and my friends again, as well as my house and garden. I'm looking forward to walking on grass and swimming in a warm ocean, but I'm also sad to leave this special place.

Antarctica is isolated, but this is probably a good thing. There has never been a war in Antarctica, and many of the world's nations cooperate in the exchange of scientific research and follow strict environmental protection policies. Antarctica is indeed unique.

Love, Bridget

# Exploration Tim

### 1772–75

Captain James Cook crossed the Antarctic Circle and discovered South Georgia and the South Sandwich Islands, but his way south was blocked by ice and he did not see Antarctica. His reports of plentiful marine life brought sealing and whaling vessels to the area.

### 1821

American sealer, John Davis, was probably the first human to set foot on Antarctica.

### 1894

An expedition led by Norwegian Henryk Bull made the first confirmed landing on Antarctica. The party discovered lichen — the first time vegetation had been found in the Antarctic region.

### 1902

Robert Falcon Scott, Ernest Shackleton, and Edward Wilson failed in an attempt to reach the South Pole.

### 1929

Commander Richard Byrd of the U.S. Navy sailed to Antarctica and built a small temporary town named Little America. Using this as his base, he flew to the South Pole.

### 1958

Using vehicles, Sir Vivian Fuchs, aided by Sir Edmund Hillary, crossed Antarctica via the South Pole.

# *Line*

## 1823

Captain James Weddell sailed further south than anyone before him and discovered a vast bay, now called Weddell Sea.

## 1831

Englishman James Clark Ross's exploration of the Arctic ignited interest in exploring Antarctica. During the next two decades, sealers and sailors would begin to map the Antarctic coast.

## 1839–43

On a four-year expedition to Antarctica, Ross discovered Victoria Land, Ross Island, the Ross Ice Shelf, and Mount Erebus.

## 1908–09

Shackleton attempted once more to reach the South Pole. He was less than 110 miles away when he had to turn back due to a lack of food. Sir Douglas Mawson, David Edgeworth, and Alistair Mackay climbed Mount Erebus.

## 1911–12

Norwegian Roald Amundsen and Robert Scott raced to be the first to reach the South Pole. Scott began his expedition with ponies from China. When the ponies died, Scott and his men had to pull their own sledges. Amundsen used huskies and reached the South Pole on December 14, 1911. Scott reached it on January 18, 1912, but his party died on their return journey.

## 1989–90

The International Trans-Antarctica Expedition led by Will Steger made the first human crossing of Antarctica using sled dogs.

## 1993

Sir Ranulph Fiennes and Dr. Michael Stroud crossed Antarctica on foot.

## 1993

Ann Bancroft (right) led the first women's team to reach the South Pole and so became the first woman to journey to both the North and South Pole.

# Glossary

**arable**     land that can be used for growing crops

**continent**     one of the seven main landmasses on earth

**crustaceans**     creatures (usually water-dwelling) with a hard exterior shell or crust

**hemisphere**     one half of the globe, above or below the equator, either the northern or southern hemisphere

**icebreaker**     a ship which has a strengthened hull specially designed to travel through ice

**insulate**     to protect against cold or heat

**nunataks**     peaks of an ice-covered mountain that show through the ice

**ozone layer**     a layer of gas in the atmosphere which helps protect the earth from harmful ultraviolet radiation

**treaty**     a signed agreement made between two or more nations

**triple-glazed**     windows made with three layers of glass – the space between each layer is designed to reduce heat loss